A DEADLY WEDDING

ASHDOWN ESTATE COZY MYSTERIES: BOOK 2

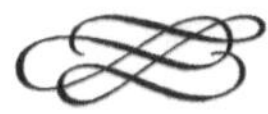

LORI WOODS

MOONSTONE PRESS

INTRODUCTION

Cecily is determined to make amends with Marianna who is still furious with her, but they have to work together to plan for the wedding of the century. The Hollands' (the richest and most influential family in the area) only son is getting married to Callista, the daughter of a waitress and a carpenter. The whole town is full of gossip with this union.

Tragedy strikes, and on the day of the wedding, the bride doesn't show up. Everyone assumes that she ran away, but when she's found murdered in her room, an investigation is opened. Cecily must out what happened and is joined by Marianna who wants to see that Callista gets justice.

Trouble seems to follow Cecily…will she be able to find the truth behind this deadly wedding, and stop the murderer in time?

CHAPTER 1

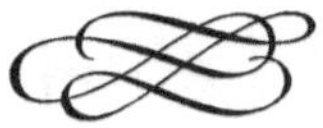

Cecily held the piping bag up high as she squeezed the buttercream frosting onto the four-tier cake in front of her. There was a deep crease between her brows as she concentrated on dressing the magnificent cake.

Each layer was moist, fresh and would melt in the mouth. She personally tasted each batch, making sure that the French Vanilla flavor came through every mouthful. Now she was on the last stretch. Getting the frosting perfect wasn't just her job, it was a matter of pride.

Her nimble fingers corrected any minor mistake and, as if by magic, the buttercream engulfed the cake and turned it into a creamy wonder.

When she was done, she took a step back and looked over at her audience.

A young woman with clear, creamy skin and auburn hair looked up at an imposing woman in a designer suit. The younger woman's expression was nervous, almost hesitant. Neither said anything for what felt like ages.

"This won't be the final outcome," Cecily explained, beginning to feel awkward. "I'll add a few more embellishments."

"I'd hope so," the older woman scoffed. "this wedding is going to be the biggest event the town has ever seen. People are expecting something more than a plain vanilla cake, Ms. Armstrong."

Cecily said nothing, but her eyes flickered over to where the young bride was standing, looking ashamed. She wanted to point out that, despite her impressive portfolio, the bride herself adamantly insisted on French Vanilla. She had a feeling that the bride was probably suffering enough.

"I'd love to hear what you have in mind," Cecily said diplomatically.

She owned a café in Brooklyn. Her skin was thicker than the average chef's, and that was an impressive boast on its own. This was hardly her first monster mother-in-law, and she doubted it would be her last. What did surprise her was that the bride seemed to crave the mother-in-law's approval, going so far as to change her wedding dress at the last second.

Cecily looked between the two of them, curiosity spilling over in her mind. It took everything she had not to burst out with a thousand questions.

The mother-in-law nodded briskly, pulling a folder from out of her enormous handbag. The bride's eyes widened slightly as she caught sight of the embossed folder. It even had its own logo with the couple's name emblazoned on the front.

'Wen Holland & Rachel Worley'

"Yes, I was at a wedding in New York last month, and they had the most incredible cake. I asked around, and I found the flavor. Oh yes, here it is."

She pulled a glossy picture out of the file and handed it to Cecily with a flourish. Cecily's eyebrows sky-rocketed and she looked at Mrs. Holland incredulously.

"Pink Champagne flavor with raspberry mousse and vanilla buttercream," Mrs. Holland said proudly, peeking over the edge of the paper.

The cake itself was a delicate pink color that lived up to its name. The delicate layers were separated by reddish-pink mousse while the entire cake was surrounded by white buttercream. The outside had delicate piping all along the sides while the top had little towers of raspberry mousse. At the center of the cake, the wedding-cake topper, a little man in a tuxedo and a bride stood proudly.

"I assume you've done something like this before?" Mrs. Holland said expectantly.

Cecily glanced up at Rachel with a questioning look, but the bride looked away carefully.

"I have," Cecily said slowly, "but the wedding's tomorrow. I'd have to work through the night to get everything done…"

Not to mention the complete waste of four tiers of perfectly good Vanilla French cake.

"Oh, wonderful," Mrs. Holland said briskly, clapping her hands. "isn't this wonderful, Rachel? I'm so glad I got here in time to make all the necessary changes. You know," she addressed Cecily. "the poor girl was in way over her head. It's overwhelming, planning a wedding fit for our family. I knew I had to get down here in time to make sure that everything was up to standard."

"At least I can still use the buttercream frosting," Cecily said, eyeing the three bowls full of expensive frosting that was sitting out on the counters.

"Oh dear," Mrs. Holland sighed. "no, no, no. That color is all wrong."

"Do you want it lighter or darker?" Cecily asked, realizing that anything she said would be disputed by the imposing woman.

"Look at the picture dear, I want it exactly like in the picture," Mrs. Holland said, narrowing her eyes at the frosting. "I think it should be lighter."

Cecily nodded slowly.

"I'll remake it all," she lied, already coming up with ways to make the frosting lighter.

"Good, now where's that other chef?" she said, looking around expectantly.

"He's taking his lunch break," Cecily said, trying not to smile in amusement.

The head chef had the foresight to disappear during Cecily's presentation. He probably knew that it was only a matter of time before Mrs. Holland set her sights on him. Cecily knew for a fact that most of the food for the wedding was ready to be cooked and sitting in the freezer. If he had to remake everything, the wedding guests would be eating cereal.

"I'll have to talk to Marianna about that," Mrs.

Holland said, pursing her lips together. "that's most unprofessional."

"He's been working non-stop on this wedding," Cecily assured her. "he's probably out getting more supplies. We know that only the best will be good enough for this wedding. And maybe not even then. We're going above and beyond."

Cecily knew that when you owned a business, it was better to gain the client's approval than make some sort of moral stand. Mrs. Holland was a pain, but she was a well-paying pain. While the head chef had the luxury of ignoring Mrs. Holland, Cecily, as partial owner of Ashdown Estate, had no choice but to smooth over ruffled feathers.

"I'd hope so," Mrs. Holland said, looking unimpressed by Cecily's little speech. "we could've gone anywhere else with our business, but we thought that the town deserved to be a part of the festivities. After all, it's not every day that the founder's son gets married."

Rachel blushed and shifted uncomfortably. Her gaze drifted over Cecily's head, and it was clear that the poor woman was barely keeping her head above water. Cecily spotted her friend, Kenna, walk into the kitchen and lean against the doorframe in amusement.

"Founder's son?" Kenna mouthed, her smile looking wicked.

"How generous," Cecily told Mrs. Holland, struggling not to crack up. "although I'm sure you've got a lot more to do today. After all, the wedding is tomorrow."

The bride seemed to snap out of her trance. She winced at the reminder but tried to hide her reaction. Unfortunately, Mrs. Holland caught on immediately and levelled her future daughter-in-law with a withering glare.

"Yes," Mrs. Holland said. "I'm glad someone sees that. Some people don't seem to appreciate our generosity. It's difficult, dealing with such ingratitude."

"I can only imagine," Cecily murmured, feeling vaguely guilty that she'd inadvertently gotten Rachel into trouble.

"We've got a lot to do today," Mrs. Holland said, grabbing hold of Rachel's elbow. "come, let's go."

With that, she all but dragged the poor young woman out of the doorway. Cecily watched them leave, her gaze full of pity for Rachel.

"Isn't she just the best?" Kenna said sarcastically, walking up to the dessert table and taking a seat.

Cecily glared hopelessly at her perfect cake. It would take forever to get Mrs. Holland's new cake right. Even then, she had a feeling that the old woman would find something to complain about.

"Well," Cecily said with a heavy sigh, slicing two generous pieces and handing one over to Kenna. "there's nothing left to do but start over. I'm sure I can repurpose this into tonight's dessert. I don't think anyone would care."

Kenna took an eager bite and rolled her eyes in bliss. She beamed over at Cecily and nodded enthusiastically.

"This doesn't even taste like plain old vanilla, it's so incredible!"

"After all this time, you still doubt me?" Cecily teased, enjoying her own slice. She grabbed the piping bag and frosted both their slices generously.

"So, what was the whole deal with the founder's son?" Kenna asked, enthusiastically digging into her mountain of frosting.

"Oh," Cecily said, rolling her eyes heavily. "that. So, the Hollands were one of the first families to settle in the town back when people were still coming over from England. They basically established the town and own most of the businesses."

"Let me guess," Kenna said, gesturing with her fork. "that makes them think they own everyone and everything."

"Technically, they do own most of the town," Cecily said in amusement. "and yes, they do think of the townspeople as their property too."

"What great people," Kenna said, rolling her eyes. "did you go to school with the fiancé? What's his name again?"

"Wen," Cecily said with a smile. "no, we were in the same year, but he went to the private school. Nigel says that he was a real pain back then too."

"Poor Rachel," Kenna said with a sigh. "I can't imagine what kind of pressure she must be under. Everyone's still talking about it. I wish they'd let it go. It's not such a big scandal."

"Are you kidding?" Cecily asked incredulously. "Her dad is a dockworker. It's like a prince marrying a servant. I don't agree with it, obviously, but people are bound to talk. With people like the Hollands, the class system never really died."

"Yeah," Kenna said fiercely. "but it should've. We're in the twenty-first century. Two people should be allowed to get married without all this prejudice. Honestly, we're not in the dark ages."

"The world's not perfect," Cecily said, shrugging her shoulders as she switched on her smart device to find the right recipe. When she finally found it, she propped her tablet in front of her and started making a list of everything she needed.

"It's sad, but Rachel had to know what she was getting herself into."

"I suppose there's worse things in life than getting married to a rich, handsome man," Kenna said with a sigh, licking frosting off a spoon.

"I just feel sorry for her. This is supposed to be her wedding, but her mother-in-law is making it difficult."

"From what I hear, it's not just the mother-in-law," Kenna said in a hushed tone. "everyone's against this wedding. The dad even spoke about disinheriting Wen, but I don't know what happened."

"What happened is none of our business," Cecily said primly. "and if I want to get done before tomorrow morning, I better get started on this cake."

"I would've told her to hire a new baker," Kenna said, leaning on her elbows and reading over the recipe. "that raspberry mousse is going to take a while."

Cecily grimaced and nodded. Thankfully, Kenna was able to help for a little while. The two of them made decent progress on the cake until Kenna had to pick up her son from his babysitter. After that, it was an uphill battle on her own.

It was around one in the morning that Cecily finally put the final touches on the cake. It took another half an hour to get a frame around it, cover the frame in cling wrap and get the cake into the industrial sized fridge.

By the time she tiredly let herself out of the kitchen, the resort was deathly quiet. Cecily hurried through the lobby to her room. As she got to the stairs, she heard an urgent voice coming through the darkness. Then, a loud sudden gasping sound.

Cecily hurried back to the lobby where she caught sight of the happy couple. Wen had Rachel's arm around his neck as he stumbled toward the staircase.

"I can't believe you did this on the night before our wedding," he hissed angrily.

Rachel giggled drunkenly and tapped his nose, before descending into a fit of laughter. He recoiled in annoyance and stumbled under her weight. She giggled again, and he looked down at her with a dark expression.

Cecily took a step back, not wanting to be spotted.

"That's enough," he said, tugging her arm roughly. "let's go."

Rachel cried out, stumbling forward painfully. She tried to pull away from him, but he pulled her against him tightly.

"You're such an embarrassment," he snapped, causing her to start crying pitifully. Even though she was drunk, the hurt was evident in her expression.

Cecily watched them go, a deep and fearful anxiety settling into her heart.

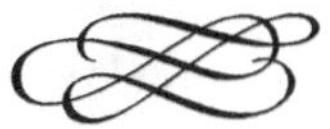

CHAPTER 2

"Cecily," Kenna gasped, looking up at the cake in awe. "you've outdone yourself. This is incredible."

The cake towered proudly over the receptionist, looking over the kitchen in all its white and reddish-pink glory. Cecily couldn't help but compare it to a bride. No, she thought to herself, it was better than that. It was a princess bride. She smiled proudly at it, smoothing down her own dress.

She got almost no sleep the previous night. Mostly because of the work she did, and partially because her mind was turning with what she'd seen. No matter what she did, she couldn't get rid of the sight of Rachel's impossibly sad expression as she stumbled to her room alongside Wen.

The look of complete disgust on his face made her stomach clench painfully. It was clear that something was very wrong, she just didn't know what to do about it. She glanced quickly at Kenna, wondering if she should share what she saw.

Her mind immediately made that decision. No. While it would be a relief to talk to someone, she felt that it wouldn't do much good. The young couple had enough going on. They didn't need more rumors added to the mix. And yet… in Cecily's heart she knew that the couple wouldn't be going through with the controversial wedding if they didn't love each other.

What she'd seen the previous night wasn't love. She wasn't sure what she'd seen, but she was sure that it wasn't a couple deeply in love with each other. What else would persuade them to get married? It wasn't as if Wen was doing it for the money. Could it be that Rachel was trying to get his family's money?

Her mind dismissed that theory. Rachel was a sweet girl. Besides, if Wen didn't truly love her, then he would've broken up with her a long time ago. Their story was romantic, but more trouble than it was worth. Why were they together if they weren't happy?

She sighed heavily as she looked up at her masterful creation. It was time to let it go. She didn't know what she saw last night, and she couldn't judge a couple off one moment. Planning a wedding was stressful. Especially this wedding. She'd probably just seen them working through it. Before her mind could argue, she shut the thought down and looked away.

"There you are," Marianna, Cecily's cousin-in-law and manager of the resort, walked in to the kitchen. Her eyes flickered over the cake, unable to hide the glimmer of amazement. Then, she looked over at Cecily and any positive emotion died. "You're late. The ceremony is about to start."

Cecily looked back at the cake longingly, then quickly followed Marianna out to the garden where the ceremony was to be held.

Wen and Rachel had chosen to get married on the topmost cliff, overlooking the ocean and the town. It was a picturesque view, but a biting wind swept over the guests. Cecily took her seat at the back, not wanting to get in anyone's way. The guest list consisted of Pleasant Valley's elite, and she knew that she wasn't particularly welcome among them.

She spotted a familiar red-head in the crowd, and smiled to herself. As if sensing her gaze, Nigel, her childhood friend, glanced over his shoulder at her and smiled widely. He waved, causing a few people to look back curiously.

A few of them glowered at Cecily, and she waved reluctantly at him. She sank into her chair, praying that he wouldn't do anything else to call attention to her. Her prayers went unanswered as Nigel stood up and fought his way out of the crowded aisle and sat down next to her.

"How's the wedding of the century treating you?" he asked with a smile.

"Just great," she groaned, trying to ignore the dirty looks she was now getting from a few of the snobbier women in town. "I had to stay up past one this morning to get that cake ready. Mrs. Holland was adamant that I remake the whole thing."

"That sounds like her," Nigel said grimly, nodding his head. "when we were back at school, she basically lived there because she was always making sure that everything was perfect for Wen."

They looked over at the future mother-in-law who was sitting proudly in the front row. A man staggered up to her, said something that made her recoil, then dropped into the seat next to her.

"Who's that?" Cecily asked, trying to see over one woman's particularly massive hat.

"That's Wen's uncle, Vince. Watch out for him. He's got a temper," Nigel said, watching Vince in amusement. "but he's also great entertainment. You never know when he's going to lose it."

Nigel had to stop talking as the music started and Wen took his place. To the casual observer, he looked as excited as anyone could be on their wedding day. To Cecily, he looked off. She noticed the slight dark circles under his eyes and how his smile was a little too wide. His eyes flickered over her, barely registering her existence.

Everyone turned expectantly to see the bride. There was nothing to see. A wave of murmurs went over the crowd and Cecily watched Wen's smile drop slightly. The music started again, but there was no-one there.

A few seconds later, an older man, presumably Rachel's father, stepped out of the greenhouse from where Rachel was supposed to make her grand entrance and shrugged his shoulders helplessly. A gasp rippled over the crowd.

Wen looked over at his mother helplessly, and an intimidating man stepped up to him. The best man looked around nervously then worriedly put his hand on Wen's shoulder. Wen shrugged him off, smiled uncomfortably at the crowd then quickly made his way over to the greenhouse. His mother smiled at the crowd too, then briskly trotted after her son.

Without thinking too hard about it, Cecily stepped aside and made her way over to Rachel's father. The man looked completely mystified and out of place in his cheap suit. As Cecily approached, she saw that he'd burned the edge of the pants while trying to iron them.

"Is everything okay?" Cecily asked sincerely. She felt Nigel step up next to her, and hoped that he wouldn't say anything to alienate the man.

"I don't know where she is," he shrugged helplessly.

A bridesmaid stepped out of the greenhouse, scowling in anger. When she spotted Mr. Worley, she stomped over.

"She still isn't here," she snapped. "are you sure you haven't seen her this morning?"

"I told you," he said in bewilderment. "I only saw her yesterday. I thought she was getting ready with you."

The bridesmaid snorted unattractively and turned on Cecily and Nigel.

"Nigel," she barked. "can you and… your friend go check up on her? She's in the Rose room."

Before anyone could say anything, she turned on her heel and went back to the greenhouse. The door slammed shut behind her, making the glass quiver in their panes.

"Trish Ferreira," Nigel explained, rolling his eyes. "she was also in our year, and let me tell you, time made her more charming."

"You mean she was worse in high school?" Cecily asked incredulously. "I can't imagine being any worse than that."

"She gets a lot worse," Mr. Worley said, narrowing his eyes at the still quivering door. "she's making poor Rachel's life a misery. Although, everyone here seems to want to do that." He looked over the crowd with a mournful expression. "I only hope Rachel makes the right decision before it's too late."

He walked away, then seated himself on a wooden bench at the back. Cecily couldn't help but feel sorry for the old man. He looked completely out of place and out of his comfort zone.

"Come on, Silly," Nigel said, draping his arm around her neck. "let's go find the missing bride. She's probably feeling nervous or whatever."

"I can't believe no-one else is going to look for her," Cecily commented, looking around at the gossiping crowd. There were at least three hundred people in attendance, but not one of them were making the move to go check on Rachel.

"Half of them bet on her running away," Nigel told her grimly. "and the other half bet on the mom shutting the whole thing down. They only care about who gets the winnings."

"Please tell me you didn't bet on her," Cecily asked in shock, turning her back on the crowd.

The manor loomed over her, drawing her in to go look for the lonely bride. As they walked, the hum of gossip grew softer. The mansion was eerily quiet, their footsteps the only sound in the empty home. The whole place was booked out for the wedding, so everyone was outside waiting for Rachel to show up.

"Are you kidding?" Nigel asked, looking at her in amusement. "I bet a fortune on mama Holland losing her mind. I would give anything to see her lose her cool."

"You're unbelievable," she joked, elbowing him lightly in the side. "don't you have any decency?"

"I don't have to have any decency," Nigel said with a playful smirk. "these are my people. If anyone deserves to mess with them, it's me."

She shook her head and rolled her eyes at him. Together, they made their way up to the Rose room. As they walked up to the door, Cecily felt a pit of dread open up in her stomach. The room was too quiet.

"I don't think anyone's up here," Nigel said, his voice becoming subdued. "I guess I owe Mitchell money."

"Is that all you care about?" Cecily asked in annoyance. She knocked on the door. The sound echoed down the hall, bouncing off the walls and coming back to them.

"Yeah," he said, frowning at her. "what else should I care about? I hardly know her, and I definitely know she can do better than Wen."

"I thought you'd stand up for your friend," Cecily teased. She was about to knock again when she thought better of it and tried the doorknob.

"He's not my friend," Nigel scoffed, rolling his eyes as he stepped into the room behind her.

The room was dark and cool, with the sound of the guests outside filtering through the open window. A light breeze drifted in, lifting the heavy curtain slightly. The room was a mess, with clothes lying everywhere. In the middle of the room, a massive four-poster bed stood in the dark, the curtains drawn.

"I'm only here because it's expected of me," Nigel continued, lightly moving some clothes out of his way as he looked around. "if I had a choice, I'd be in town watching movies with you."

His words drifted to the background as Cecily approached the bed, her pulse pounding in her ears. Something felt very wrong.

"This room's empty. I think she did the smart thing and left. I'll be honest, if I were in her shoes then I'd do the same."

Cecily ignored him, took hold of one edge of the curtain and yanked it to the side. Nigel swore loudly and stumbled back while Cecily looked down in horror.

There, concealed by the curtains around her bed, was Rachel. She lay impossibly still, looking like the perfect bride, dressed in a gorgeous gown, her angelic face covered by the expensive lace veil.

CHAPTER 3

"So," the police captain said, surveying the scene from behind his dark sunglasses. "where do you think we should start?"

The wedding guests had drifted off and were grouped into small clumps of people all across the resort. Some had retired to their rooms, not wanting to get involved in the inevitable investigation, while others milled around curiously, waiting to see what happened.

Nigel had disappeared once the news broke, opting to offer his condolences then get out of the way. Cecily understood his actions. They'd all had enough involvement with the police when they were teenagers. She knew her childhood friend better than anyone. Nigel hated drama and tried to avoid it as much as possible.

Now, she was standing outside with the handsome police captain, Adam Somers. He was fairly new to the town and despite their surly first meeting, he proved to be a real ally.

Cecily shrugged her shoulders, looking over the guests. She had no idea where to begin. If rumors were to be believed, everybody wanted Rachel gone. A marriage between classes was the stuff of romance novels, but it was much messier in real life.

Wen and his family were holed up in their suite, trying to come to terms with what had happened, while Rachel's family were huddled up in the dining room. Any time people came close, they'd bare their teeth to make it clear they weren't welcome. It was as if the resort was a battleground, with two opposing camps biding their time.

It was an explosive situation that they needed to resolve before war broke out. Cecily chewed on her thumb nail, looking around her thoughtfully.

The answer came to her all at once. Trish Ferreira sashayed past, looking suitably upset. This didn't stop her from soaking up all the attention that fell on her as the maid-of-honor. Cecily narrowed her eyes at the woman as she tearfully told an older man how distressed she was.

"I think we should start with her," Cecily said quickly, discreetly pointing at Trish. "I met her earlier, and there seemed to be a bit of friction there. Besides, she was probably the last person who saw Rachel."

Adam looked over at her thoughtfully then nodded slowly.

"I guess I'm not going to get rid of you until this thing is solved?" he asked in amusement as he started forward and she followed him.

"You asked my opinion," she reminded him seriously. "there's no going back now."

"No," he said, looking down at her thoughtfully. "I don't think there is."

She spotted him looking at her, blushed slightly and focused back on Trish. As they approached, they heard a few snippets of her conversation.

"It's so awfully tragic," Trish said, her voice breaking slightly. "I don't think she could handle the pressure. It's not easy, especially since she was so unprepared for all of this."

"I'm guessing planning a wedding of this size isn't all glitz and glamour?" Adam commented, stepping up to them and inserting himself in the conversation.

Trish looked at him haughtily, glancing at his uniform and raising an eyebrow. She seemed to want to say something snappy, then thought the better of it and closed her mouth.

"You've got no idea what goes into this sort of thing," Trish said firmly. "it's not any wedding. It can't be ordinary. Unfortunately, Rachel didn't have the taste to pull something like this off. If it weren't for me and Lara, then this would've been an embarrassment."

"Instead, it turned out to be a tragic event," Adam said slowly, not slowing down to ask who Lara was.

Cecily was about to ask, but he gave her a warning look. She nodded stiffly, coming to the conclusion that Lara was Wen's mother. She never thought to ask Mrs. Holland her first name. The woman never took a breath when talking to staff. She steamrolled them, then clicked away in her expensive heels. None of them were inclined to get on a first-name basis with the Holland family dragon.

"It's not our fault this happened," Trish said primly, flipping her black hair over her shoulder.

"Rachel should've backed out sooner if she was having trouble keeping up."

"Hold on," Cecily said slowly. "do you think that Rachel killed herself?"

Trish frowned at her. The old man she'd been talking to melted away awkwardly, sensing that he wasn't welcome. As he went, he gave Trish a concerned look. From the looks of things, he was already telling people that Trish was a person of interest in the case. Trish kept glancing around fearfully, knowing that rumors were spreading as they stood there.

"Well," Trish flipped her hair again awkwardly. "what else would it be? She was alone the whole time, and it makes sense. Rachel was a bit of a drama-queen. I mean the whole dying in her wedding dress is just so awfully tragic. It's just too perfect, it was obviously planned."

"Yes, it was planned," Adam nodded somberly. "but not by her. Rachel was murdered. The medical examiner confirmed it as soon as he got here."

"No way," Trish gasped, her eyes widening. "who do you think did it? Do you think the murderer could be here right now?"

She looked around suspiciously, her expression more curious than sad.

"How long did you know Rachel?" Cecily asked, changing the subject quickly.

"Not long," Trish said, examining her nails thoughtfully. "I think we met about six months ago when Wen introduced her to the family."

"Are you friends with the family?" Adam asked.

"Yeah," Trish said, looking at him incredulously. "it's common knowledge. You should really know these things."

Adam frowned at her and opened his mouth to say something. While it wasn't his job to know all the personal relationships of people in town, it would've been helpful to know what happened among Pleasant Valley's elite. Cecily looked up at him, feeling a swell of pride.

The previous police captain was infamously close with the wealthy families in town. Whenever they needed help, they'd call him, and he'd make the problem go away. This sort of bias caused all sorts of trouble, especially when one of the poorer families got on the wrong side of one of the elite families.

Cecily couldn't prove anything, but she knew for a fact that her own uncle had the previous police captain in his pocket. It was a relief to know that history wasn't repeating itself with Adam.

She wasn't the only one who was surprised and detected a strange emotion on Trish's face. It was clear that she was used to a different kind of treatment from public officials.

"You two must've really hit it off," Cecily said, coming to Adam's rescue. "Rachel must've really liked you if she chose you to be her maid-of-honor."

"Oh please, she had no choice," Trish rolled her eyes. "it was decided from the moment they were engaged. Like a lot of other things. When you marry into a family like this one, you've got to accept a few things. Rachel never really understood that."

"It looks like she did, if she made you her maid-of-honor," Cecily pointed out.

"You didn't hear this from me," Trish said, lowering her voice and stepping closer to them. "but she wasn't happy about any of this. When Lara came to make those changes yesterday, Rachel had a meltdown in her room. Wen tried his best to calm her down, but things didn't end well."

Cecily and Adam shared a troubled look. Before they could ask her what she meant, a handsome man walked up to them with an anxious expression. When he stood next to Trish, it was clear to see they were related. They shared the same olive-toned skin, dark eyes and midnight black hair. They made an arresting pair.

Cecily recognized the new arrival as the best man. She felt vaguely sorry for the groom. It wouldn't have been easy standing next to someone who made him look small and pudgy by comparison. She could just see the pictures now. The gorgeous bridal party and the plain groom.

"Hey," he said, holding his hand out for Adam to shake. "I just heard that Rachel was murdered. Is it true?"

"I'm afraid so," Adam said grimly. "we'll be asking all the guests a couple of questions."

"This is my brother, Doug," Trish said, looking at him in annoyance. "he's Wen's best man."

"Are the two of you actually best friends, or was that another position that was filled because of tradition?" Adam asked curiously.

"No, they've been close since they were kids," Trish said, waving her hand dismissively.

"Yeah, and Wen's a real mess about this whole thing," he said gravely. "whatever you guys need help with, just let me know."

"We were just talking about Rachel buckling under the pressure yesterday," Trish said, putting her hand on her hip and looking around. Her anxiety about being a person of interest seemed to disappear when she realized that everyone was looking at them.

"That wasn't great," Doug admitted, wincing as he remembered it.

"You were there?" Cecily asked in surprise. "It doesn't seem like the type of argument that would happen in front of other people."

"Wen wasn't happy about it," Doug said with a sigh, "but she just lost it. I think she'd been holding it in for so long that she couldn't stop once it started."

"Can you tell us what happened?" Adam asked with concern.

"I'll tell you what happened," Trish said, interjecting before Doug could say anything. "she went crazy. She was just screaming at him and throwing things. It was so embarrassing."

"Trish," Doug said with a frown. "have some sympathy. She was under a lot of pressure. It wasn't fair of Wen to leave her to the wolves like that. He knew how difficult it was for her, but he didn't do anything to help her."

"She should've been stronger," Trish said, shrugging her shoulders unapologetically. "she was only with him because she thought he was an easy target. If she wanted the fortune, she should've been strong enough to take on the family."

"You think Rachel was only with Wen to get the money?" Adam interrupted before she could get off topic.

"It's obvious," Trish looked at him as though he were stupid. "say what you want about her, but she was gorgeous. Look at Wen, if it weren't for the money, she probably wouldn't have even looked at him."

"Come on, Trish," Doug said in disgust. "that's harsh."

"You know it's true," she said, wrinkling her nose. "Wen's been trying to get married for years. He tried his luck with all of us, but he's a little weasel. He couldn't get anyone decent, so he got desperate and fell for that little gold digger."

"You don't think they were in love?" Cecily asked, feeling saddened on behalf of the couple.

"They certainly didn't look it," Trish scoffed, raising an eyebrow. "you know what she did when she finished her little tantrum? She went out drinking and came home who knows how late. Wen had to go drag her out of some hole-in-the-wall. It was embarrassing. Tell me, what happy bride-to-be is going to spend the night before her wedding getting drunk with strangers on the dock?"

"Wasn't her dad a dockworker?" Cecily asked thoughtfully. "Maybe she knew the people there and wanted to go somewhere she was comfortable."

"Obviously she should've stayed there," Trish said venomously. "look, are we done here? I've got things to do."

"Just one more thing," Adam said, holding up a hand to stop her from leaving. "when did you last see Rachel?"

"I left her with the stylists this morning, then came down to the greenhouse to drink," Trish said with a grin. "ask Doug, a whole bunch of us were down here making bets on whether or not she'd make a break for it."

Doug nodded, looking intensely ashamed as he stared down at the ground with his cheeks turning a vibrant red.

"If you want to talk to anyone about what happened, ask Wen where he disappeared to at about ten this morning."

CHAPTER 4

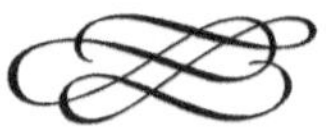

They knocked on Wen's door and waited patiently for him to open. It had taken them a while to find someone who knew where he was. Apparently, as soon as he found out what happened to Rachel, he walked away without telling anyone where he was going.

After asking a few of the guests with no success, Cecily went inside and asked one of the maids to help find out where he was. Within a few minutes, the maid came back and confirmed that he had shut himself in his room.

They knocked again, more insistently this time. After a few seconds, they heard someone shuffling inside, and the door opened to reveal Wen. His expression was stricken, and he stared at them with wide eyes. He looked right past them, as if he wasn't really seeing them.

Then, he turned away, leaving the door open as he went and curled up on one of the couches.

"Mr. Holland?" Adam asked, peeking into the room curiously. "do you mind if we ask you a few questions about your fiancée?"

"Is it true?" he croaked, his voice harsh and raspy.

"Is what true?" Cecily asked compassionately, stepping through the doorway and looking at him in concern. She sat down on the couch opposite him, watching him carefully.

"That someone killed her," Wen said, looking at her intently.

She shifted uncomfortably in her seat, suddenly wishing that she hadn't chosen to sit across from him. His clear blue eyes were fixed on her, and he wouldn't look away, no matter how uncomfortable she got. Eventually, she looked up to meet his gaze to see if it would make things better.

Wen wasn't a hunk. He'd never make it onto the cover of magazines, and he wouldn't stand out in a crowd. And yet, she couldn't see why Trish called him a weasel. With his blue eyes and clear skin, he was attractive in a mild sort of way.

While he wouldn't be pulling in crowds of women, he probably wouldn't have trouble finding someone.

"I'm afraid it is," she said sympathetically, nodding slowly and looking away.

He groaned like a dying animal, then lay himself down and turned on his side. He looked up at the ceiling, his eyes filling with tears. Cecily looked at Adam with a confused expression, and he shrugged his shoulders.

"I'm sorry to do this to you now, but is there anything you can tell us to help us?" Adam asked, watching him cautiously and sitting down on the edge of the couch next to Cecily.

Wen ignored him and shook his head as the tears streamed down his cheeks. Adam looked at Cecily, confusion coloring his expression. This was a strange reaction, and neither of them were sure how to handle it. It looked sincere, but it was also one of the strangest things they'd ever seen.

Cecily's mind wandered back to how Lara treated her the previous day, and she pursed her lips with determination.

"Wen," she said firmly, standing up and putting her hands on her hips. "this isn't working. Sit up and talk to us."

Wen looked at her unseeingly, so she walked

up to him, pulled him up and fixed him with a haughty glare. He narrowed his eyes at her but sniffed and sat up. She looked back at Adam in surprise, not believing that it actually worked.

"What do you want from me?" he asked, wiping his nose with his sleeve. "Can't you see I'm upset?"

"Yeah, we all are," Cecily said unsympathetically, channeling her inner Mrs. Holland. "you need to help us find out who did this, or else things will get worse."

"I don't know what to tell you," Wen said, shrugging helplessly.

"Why don't we start with this morning," Adam said, giving Cecily a warning look. "someone said that you went to see her at about ten in the morning. How was she at that time?"

"I don't know," Wen said, shrugging pathetically. "I didn't see her. When I got to her room, she was already gone. One of the maids said she got a call then walked outside."

It turned out that asking the maids was an effective way to find anything out in the hotel. Cecily made a mental note of this, knowing that it could come in handy in the future.

"I went outside to find her, but she was standing at the edge of the property."

"Why didn't you go up and talk to her?" Cecily asked with a frown.

"She was in her wedding dress," Wen said, looking scandalized. "it's bad luck for the groom to see the bride in her…" he trailed off, his eyes opening wide in realization. "this is my fault. Oh… this is all my fault."

He buried his face in his hands and let out a long moan. Adam looked startled, while Cecily tried to hide any emotion in case he looked up.

"You think this is your fault because you saw her in her wedding dress?" Cecily clarified, trying to hide her incredulous tone.

"Yes!" he cried, shaking his head vigorously. "Isn't it obvious? None of this would've happened if I stayed put. We would've been married now."

"Okay," Adam said slowly. "did she seem upset to you? Do you have any idea of who she was talking to?"

"I don't know," Wen shook his head again. "I don't know who would call her. Everyone she knows is here. She was all the way at the edge of the woods. I thought her dress was going to get muddy. I've got no idea why she'd do that in her wedding dress."

"How did she seem?" Adam asked urgently,

sensing that Wen was starting to lose his ratio-
nality again.

Unfortunately, he was too late. Wen let out a loud groan again and sank into the couch, closing his eyes. Cecily towered over him but knew that her trick wouldn't work again. She turned to look at Adam, who shrugged and gestured toward the door. She nodded, and the two of them walked out, leaving Wen to his strange grieving process.

"I don't get it," Cecily said in frustration. "one source says that the couple didn't look in love and that Rachel wasn't happy. But then we talk to Wen, and he's obviously heartbroken. They must've been in love, why else would Rachel put herself through so much trouble?"

"Life's weird," Adam said with a casual shrug. "and so is love. Maybe they were in love, or maybe something else is going on."

"That's real helpful," Cecily said sarcastically. "perfect policework right there."

"What do you want me to say?" He asked, looking down at her in amusement. "They were madly in love but acted weird because they were on drugs or something? I don't know anything about these people. All I know is what other people are telling me. We probably won't know by the end of this either. Some things are a mystery. I'm not here to figure out if they were in love."

"She was murdered at her own wedding," Cecily reminded him. "I think questioning their relationship is the perfect place to start."

"That's what literally every other person at this wedding is saying," Adam pointed out with a smirk. "maybe we should be focusing on the facts."

"Whatever," Cecily said with a shrug. "I still think we should be looking for motive."

"You can't convict a person on motive," Adam pointed out. "we need to find some cold, hard evidence if we want to arrest anyone."

Cecily nodded, opening her mouth to say something when someone called her name. They turned around to see Marianna stomping up to them furiously.

"What do you think you're doing?" she asked, putting her arms over her chest and glaring at her cousin-in-law.

"I'm looking for a murderer," Cecily said with a shrug.

There was a time when Cecily held out hope that she and Marianna could be close. The events from fifteen years earlier had ostracized Cecily from the rest of her family and she hoped that

Marianna could be her link back. Unfortunately, Marianna didn't like her.

At first, it hurt Cecily and she tried her best to make amends. Eventually, she figured out that some people were set in their ways and that no amount of niceness was going to change their mind. With that sobering thought, she stood up to her cousin and laid down the law. Cecily was tired of being treated as a second-class citizen in her childhood home.

"That's not your job," Marianna hissed, narrowing her eyes at her. "you're part owner of this place, you should be helping me calm our guests down. You shouldn't be out here walking around in the mud. You're ruining my lawn!"

"It's my lawn too," Cecily reminded her, rolling her eyes. "and I think the best way to calm the guests down is if we figure out what happened to the bride. If you're so worried about them, go calm them down yourself."

Wit that, she turned to Adam and nodded at him. They walked off, and Cecily clenched her eyes closed hoping that Marianna would leave well enough alone.

"You insisted on becoming a partner in the business, and I expect you to pull your weight," Marianna said furiously.

They got to the edge of the forest and looked around. Cecily did her best to try and ignore her business partner. Unfortunately, Marianna wasn't going to be ignored.

"What are you doing?"

Cecily quickly found Rachel's footprints and it was all thanks to the weather. It had been raining on and off for a few days, soaking the lavish grass and causing people to sink into the soft ground and pull up the grass as they walked. Because of this, people had avoided walking on the grass ever since the rains began.

Rachel was probably the only guest who made her way up the hill to the edge of the forest. Cecily raised her eyebrows as she thought. It must've been a very important phone call to get her to make the trek in her wedding dress. She could only imagine the consequences if she showed up to the ceremony with even a droplet of mud on the brilliant white designer gown. She was sure that Rachel was well aware of the consequences too.

The only question was, who was important enough to get her to face Mrs. Holland's wrath? Everyone Rachel and Wen loved would've been at the wedding ceremony, and most people were accounted for as they arrived. She thought back, realizing that most guests had mud on their shoes. That was one of the perils of having a wedding outdoors.

"Will one of you answer me?" Marianna huffed. "This is ridiculous. Do you know what the Hollands are going to do to us? They could ruin the business."

"They won't do that," Cecily said, closing her eyes in annoyance. She wished Marianna would go back to the mansion. "we didn't kill Rachel. Besides, they want answers as soon as possible. The sooner we get this done, the less of a scandal it will be for them."

"Unless one of them did it," Adam muttered under his breath.

They scanned the ground carefully, looking for a second set of footprints. As they got to the edge of the forest, the grass disappeared somewhat, leaving behind only open ground. Cecily's mouth dropped open as she looked at the mess in front of her.

The ground was overturned, with no discernible footprints.

"It looks like someone had a fight," Cecily said, looking at Adam with despair.

"Yeah," Adam said grimly, getting down to his haunches and surveying the scene. "and we can't

see where it started or ended. But I'll bet you anything that this is where she died."

"Oh, for heaven's sake," Marianna exclaimed
loudly, causing Cecily to grimace in annoyance.
"who's been smoking out here?"

They looked around in surprise to find Marianna holding up a single cigarette butt in disgust.

"One of my deputies is taking the evidence to the lab for testing," Adam said, putting his phone in his pocket and looking around at the women in front of them.

After Marianna found the cigarette butt, he quickly bagged the evidence and got the deputies on the phone. Now, they were all standing in Marianna's fancy office, dripping water all over her expensive carpet.

Cecily looked around the room, remembering it as her uncle's office. She and her cousin, JR, were never allowed in the room. Once or twice, they snuck in when they were bored, convinced that JR's father must be up to something exciting and mysterious. Why else would he keep them out of his office with such religious fervor?

She felt sorry for her uncle. It must've been difficult trying to find some peace and quiet in a house with the two of them running around amok. They never did find anything interesting in the office. It was clearly just his escape from the world.

Marianna had done a lot of remodeling, so much that she barely recognized the room anymore. Her uncle appreciated old-world luxury. His idea of a well-decorated room included his hunting trophies and heavy wooden furniture. He also kept his liquor cabinet well-stocked, which the teenage cousins took as a blessing. Once they were older, they snuck in regularly to see what they could score.

Marianna had ripped everything out except the hardwood floor. It was now a sleek, modern room that bore little resemblance to its former self. Cecily couldn't blame her. It had been a stuffy room that died when her aunt and uncle left the mansion for good.

As always, her mind drifted to the summer she turned sixteen. Once the most traumatic experience of her life happened, her family couldn't bear to live under a cloud of scandal. They sent

JR to a private school and left the country. Her father left to conduct some business in a different city, while Cecily was left alone in an empty house with the housekeeper.

Standing in her uncle's old office was bittersweet. It reminded her of the better times she had with her family, but it was also satisfying knowing that nothing of her uncle's presence remained. In this room, at least, everything was new.

"How long until we get results?" Cecily asked, leaning against the windowsill, watching the rain pour outside.

While they were still outside, the skies had opened up a flood over their heads. Everyone who'd been left outside to gossip and speculate immediately ran for cover. Cecily winced when she thought of what the main lobby would look like after everyone ran through with their muddy footprints.

The rain would also do a good job of washing away any trail that was left at the end of the footpath. When they went back, everything would be fresh and clean. Usually this made Cecily smile, but this time it meant that any evidence at the crime scene was slowly degrading or being swept away.

She couldn't help but think that the murderer had mother nature on their side. This thought made her purse her lips grimly. Even so, nothing would stop her from finding out who murdered the friendless bride.

As she turned to look at Adam, she couldn't help but notice Marianna's troubled expression. Her cousin-in-law was nervously biting the inside of her cheek.

"It could be weeks," Adam admitted with a weak shrug. "these things take time. The labs are always swamped with work."

"Weeks?" Marianna asked in shock. "We can't wait that long. Don't they know who was murdered?"

"That's not exactly their concern," Adam told her firmly. "they deal with this kind of thing every day. We have to wait our turn like everyone else."

"We need answers now," Marianna said, obviously troubled. "we can't let this sort of scandal hang over us for that long. It's bad for business."

"Forgive me if that's not my main priority," Adam said, looking unmoved. "unless people come forward with information, my hands are tied. Science works, but it takes time."

Marianna leaned back in her leather chair

with a frown. She chewed on her cheek again, looking out the window thoughtfully.

"What kind of information?" she asked eventually.

"Anything from seeing her do something strange to actually seeing someone kill her," Adam said, looking at her intently. "witnesses are very important in a case like this. Sometimes they're how we get anything done."

Marianna sighed heavily, then shook her head.

"I think I might know something," she said eventually.

Cecily tilted her head in surprise and curiosity. She quickly looked over at Adam, realizing that this was his goal the whole time. The corners of his lips quirked up, and he leaned forward subconsciously.

"What is it?" Cecily asked gently.

"The family never really wanted Rachel around," Marianna said with a heavy sigh. "that was common knowledge, but the uncle was the most vocal about it. People say that he was bullying her to try and get her to leave. I saw it happen once or twice."

"And you believe that he was capable of murdering his niece-to-be?" Adam asked, rubbing his chin skeptically.

Marianna nodded slowly, looking down at her hands. Cecily's breath caught in her throat and she shook her head sadly.

"Do you have something to say?" Marianna barked.

"No," Cecily said, in annoyance. "I guess minding your business means turning a blind eye to someone in need."

Marianna scoffed and rolled her eyes. Adam gave Cecily a warning look, and she pressed her lips into a thin line. This town and its people had a way of getting under her skin. It was home but it was flawed.

"Do you know where we can find the uncle?"

"He's probably at the bar," Marianna said, shrugging lightly. "he's got a bit of a problem." She made a drinking motion with her hand and winced.

With that charming visual in their minds, it wasn't hard to find the uncle. Vince was sitting alone at the corner of the antique bar. He nursed a whiskey and stared broodingly into the distance in a way that let them know it wasn't his first drink.

"Mind if we sit here?" Cecily asked, pulling a

bar stool out and sitting before he could answer. He looked at her in annoyance but didn't say anything.

Adam sat on his other side and gestured to the bartender.

"I'll get you guys whatever you want," the bartender said, approaching them warily, "but this guy," he pointed at Vince, "has been cut off."

"I can drink whatever I want, whenever I want," Vince growled, glaring venomously at the poor server.

"That's your deal, buddy, but you won't do that here," the server said, raising an eyebrow.

Cecily felt sorry for the bartender but knew that he'd be able to handle himself. If there was one occupation that Cecily respected, it was bartenders. They had to have a wide range of skills to succeed at their job. It took a special person to return to the craziness they had to face every day.

From the bartender's expression, she could tell that he was experienced with Vince's type. People tended to become their worst self when they had a few drinks in. That meant that bartenders had to work with the worst side of human nature every day and find a way to be civil.

"Oh, come on," Vince whined, "give me a break. Someone died, man."

"From what we heard, we thought you'd be celebrating," Cecily quipped, leaning on the bar and watching the interaction with interest.

"Yeah," the bartender said, raising an eyebrow. "we all know you hated the girl."

Vince shrugged, taking a large swig of his drink. He drank in a way that made it clear that he didn't take the bartender's warning too seriously.

"Death is death," Vince said, slurring slightly. "the girl was a gold digger, and she got her payment earlier than expected."

He giggled at his own incoherent joke, raising his glass as if to toast something, not caring how the liquid sloshed out of his glass. A few drops landed on Adam, which he brushed off in annoyance.

"I mean it, dude," the bartender said sternly. "your brother said I can't let you get past five drinks. You're at the limit."

"My brother should be here," Vince said, looking around blearily. "he just saved a million dollars."

"Good business deal?" Cecily asked curiously.

"Nah," Vince leaned toward her and lowered

his voice conspiratorially. "he was going to offer the little hussy a million dollars to leave his son alone."

"Wasn't that a bit late?" Cecily asked with a frown. "They were about to get married. Shouldn't he have done that a lot earlier?"

"He did," Vince hiccupped. "but she said no. Then, yesterday, she asked if she could meet up with him. They were supposed to meet before the wedding, but it looks like James lucked out. That boy's lucky too."

"Do you mean Wen?" Cecily asked, looking over at Adam with wide eyes.

"The very same," Vince nodded, his eyes looking unfocused as he burped inside his mouth. "his good ol' daddy woulda got that money back from him somehow. Trust me, you don't want to owe James Holland a million dollars. He'll make you pay him back with *your soul.*"

Vince whispered the last two words as if he was telling her a secret.

"How would you know?" Cecily asked slowly. "Do you owe your brother money?"

Vince leaned back and watched her suspiciously. He sipped his drink, nearing the bottom of the glass with one big gulp. The bartender watched him carefully, slowly putting everything down and crossing his arms over his chest.

"Everyone owes James something," Vince said with a forced laugh. "show me one person in this town that doesn't have debt with James Holland, and I'll show you a liar."

Cecily raised an eyebrow in surprise and leaned back in her stool as she processed the information. She looked over at Adam, unsure about what to do next.

"Do you know if James ended up meeting with Rachel this morning?" Adam asked, trying to get Vince's attention.

The drunk man looked over at him in annoyance. He took another sip, but it wasn't enough to fill his mouth. He looked down at the empty glass and waved it at the bartender.

"I told you," the bartender said, lifting his chin. "you're not getting anymore. You're cut off."

"Yeah, whatever," Vince scoffed, "just put it on my brother's tab."

"No," the bartender said, his voice steely. "I can't. Your brother made it very clear that five drinks was your limit. And by the looks of things, you probably started long before you got here."

"I don't need you," Vince scoffed angrily. "I can get a drink myself."

With those strong words, Vince heaved himself up with great effort and leaned over the bar trying to reach the drinks.

"Stop that," the bartender said, quickly snatching away anything alcoholic. He held the bottles away from Vince, setting them on the inner counter.

"Give me the bottle," Vince said, his blubbery face getting red. He was bent at the waist, with his whole stomach and torso leaning over the bar. His feet kicked slightly as he tried to get himself closer to the alcohol bottle.

The bartender stepped backward in annoyance.

"Get back or I'll call security," he threatened.

"Call security!" Vince shouted. "I'll show them! I'll show you!"

Vince now tried to climb over the bar, his intent clear. Adam quickly grabbed onto the back of the man's shirt and pulled him back while the bartender snatched a broom stick and brandished it threateningly.

"Let me go!" Vince shouted, his face turning a shade of purple. "Let me go!" He swung his fists around, his expression murderous.

CHAPTER 6

By the time they managed to calm Vince down, most of the hotel had heard the sound of his screaming. It must've been a common occurrence because when Adam led a seething Vince to a private room, onlookers seemed unsurprised.

Cecily saw one or two guests poke their heads around the door, but when they saw who the source of the commotion was, they just rolled their eyes and walked away.

They also didn't manage to calm him down completely. His hands were shaking in the cuffs that Adam snapped around his wrists. He glared at Cecily as though she were personally to blame for all the misfortune he was experiencing. She lifted her chin defiantly and narrowed her eyes at him.

Cecily led them back to Marianna's office. The poor hotel manager's mouth dropped open when a ruffled Adam barged in dragging an unwilling drunk behind him. Cecily managed an apologetic smile before helping Adam get Vince down on a chair.

"Sorry about the intrusion," Adam said, puffing slightly. He straightened up and moved a piece of hair away from his forehead before giving Marianna a charming smile. "we didn't know where else to take him."

Marianna looked dumbstruck at Adam's affecting smile, then shook her head silently. Her eyes flickered over to where Vince was quietly seething.

"I could sue you over this," Vince said, grinding his teeth angrily.

"Now, why would you want to do that?" Adam asked, looking affronted.

"You arrested me," Vince sputtered, his eyes clouding with confusion.

He looked around for support, but Marianna shook her head and sat down again while Cecily looked curiously at Adam. He grinned at her before giving her a cheeky wink. He turned to their suspect and moved a chair so that he could sit facing him.

"I didn't arrest you," Adam said easily. "that would be illegal. I just wanted to help you calm down. Do you feel calmer now?"

Vince glared at him suspiciously, then nodded his head slowly. His eyes flickered back to Marianna, but she busied herself with some paperwork. Cecily leaned against Marianna's desk, her back toward her cousin-in-law. She studied Vince carefully, her nose wrinkling slightly.

For someone who professed to be proud of his family, Vince didn't seem to possess any pride for himself. His clothes were expensive but wrinkled and dirty. His skin was starting to sag while his nose was becoming bulbous from too much drink.

There were whispers of a handsome man behind the alcoholic wreck that he'd become. Compared to his brother, the handsome patriarch of the Holland family, it was clear that Vince was a disappointment. He seemed to realize this as he sank low in his chair, looking sullenly at the people around him.

"Well?" Adam prompted, looking him over curiously.

Vince sighed heavily before nodding. He kept

his gaze averted and his shoulders slumped around him as the drink began to wear off.

"I think you could use a few more minutes," Adam said conversationally, "we'll be back later. Just to give you some time to cool off."

He walked over to the door, gesturing for Cecily to follow him. Marianna looked up in surprise and made a sound of protest at the back of her throat.

"You can't leave him in here," she said, looking incredulous. "I've got work to do."

"We've got nowhere else to leave him," Cecily said, trying to communicate through her expression, but Marianna was clueless.

"Take him to his room," she said, gesturing at him in annoyance. "he's paying enough for it."

"No," Adam said, smiling in amusement. "I don't think we'd get him up the stairs in those cuffs. Keep an eye on him, won't you?"

Before Marianna could say a word, they were out the door. She breathed out in annoyance and looked over at Vince. He shrugged helplessly at her.

"We've got some time," Adam said with a smile. "what do you think we should do with it?"

Cecily smiled at him, then furrowed her brow

thoughtfully. She pursed her lips slightly, then a thought hit her.

"What if we search his room?" she suggested. "He can't hide anything now, and we probably won't get another chance like this."

"I don't have a search warrant," he pointed out. "anything I find would be thrown out if we took this to trial."

"What do you need to get a warrant?"

"I need to go to a judge with probable cause."

"Which is going to be difficult since the Holland family is close to the only judge in the area," Cecily realized, rolling her eyes in annoyance. She crossed her arms over her chest as they stood outside. Suddenly, she straightened up as though something hit her.

"What?" he asked, amused by her transparency.

One of Cecily's biggest flaws was that everything she thought was immediately written on her face. It was a struggle to try and control it, because people could either get offended or laugh at her. Right now, her eyes were wide and sparkling with her mouth a little agape. She smiled mischievously at him, dropping her chin a little so that she was looking at him from under her lashes.

"I'm not a cop," she said, gesturing to herself. "what if I found probable cause? Then the judge would have to give you that warrant."

"How are we going to keep him out of his room until the judge signs off on the warrant?" Adam asked, rubbing his chin thoughtfully.

"If you've got probable cause, then you could probably just keep him from going in," Cecily said with a shrug.

"And how are you going to find probable cause?" Adam asked, raising an eyebrow at her.

"It's probably best if you don't know," Cecily told him, still grinning. She poked him in the chest with her forefinger, then quickly hurried away.

"I don't like where this is going," he called after her, scratching the back of his head nervously.

"There's cake in the kitchen," she said over her shoulder. "you should try some!"

One of the perks of co-owning the resort was that she had a master key for every door. She had every right to go into the room, but she still looked around nervously before letting herself into Vince's room.

Her heart was beating a mile a minute, and she felt nervous energy flood her limbs. This was the first time she'd ever snuck into someone's room before. The feeling was exhilarating. She closed the door softly behind her then turned to look at the dirtiest room she'd ever seen.

Although Vince only checked in two days ago, his room was a pigsty. There were empty bottles and takeaway packets strewn all over the place. His suitcase was still sitting on the expensive dresser, it was half-open with all his clothes spilling out.

She imagined that whenever he wanted to wear something, he tossed everything out of his bag then kicked the clothes around until he found something clean. The heavy curtains were still shut, and the whole room had an unpleasant odor that crept into her lungs and caused her to close her nose tightly, hardly daring to breathe.

Cecily fumbled with her phone then quickly put on the flashlight. The light only made the mess worse as it caused shadows to jump out at her. She winced as she tried to disturb the mess as little as possible. Although, she doubted Vince would notice anything, the way things were arranged.

It was a slow trek making her way over the messy terrain, and she nearly tripped over a pair of jeans that had been left near the door. She quickly caught herself on one of the bed's posters, but as she righted herself, she saw something strange under the bed.

Taking a deep breath, she bent down and examined the item. Her eyes widened when she realized what she was looking at. There, lying at the corner of the bed, was part of a heavy branch. What made it stand out to her was the fact that it was lying in a puddle of dark red blood.

She spun around, her flashlight illuminating the path to the door. It was easy to see Vince's movements from earlier that day. His dress shoes were a few paces apart, indicating that he walked into the room and stepped them off using his toes. His expensive dress jacket was tossed onto one corner of the bed. She saw him sit down on the edge of the bed, dropping the branch as he shrugged himself out of his jacket.

Cecily imagined him walking to the bathroom, washing his hands, then using a white hotel towel to wipe the red streaks off his hands. The tell-tale red streaked white towel lay next to one of the chairs.

It only took a few seconds to snap a few pictures on her phone before she quickly made her way out of the room. As she walked, it became more than a messy room. The atmosphere became oppressive and it felt like someone was watching her. She shivered as she looked back quickly, her eyes trying to reassure her that she was safe.

Unfortunately, the hairs at the back of her neck were standing on edge, and it took everything she had not to run out of the room like a little child. She quickly let herself out, then all but jogged down to the kitchen.

As she passed the security room, her steps slowed. The door was slightly ajar, and she noticed someone moving around in the room. She peeked around the corner and spotted a security guard lazily watching screens in front of him.

"Hey," she said, leaning against the door frame. "do you think you could help me with something?"

It occurred to them to watch the security footage earlier, but since there weren't any cameras near the reception venue or where Rachel was killed, the idea didn't have much priority. Everything changed now that she suspected something happened in Vince's room. And maybe she'd be able to figure out how the murderer moved Rachel's body from the murder scene to the room.

She also wondered briefly why the murderer

went through so much trouble to arrange Rachel in her room. Surely it would've been easier to leave her at the edge of the forest. Or even hide her in the forest. Why take the risk to arrange the bride in her room?

The security guard pulled up the right footage for the day, but when he pressed play, the footage jumped on the screen then glitched and went back to an hour earlier. They looked at each other in alarm.

"What does that mean?" Cecily asked with wide eyes.

"I don't know," he said, his voice holding a slight edge of panic. "I think we were hacked."

He tried it again, but the same thing happened. When he tried a third time, Cecily held out her hand to stop him.

"I don't think we're going to fix it like that," she said, shaking her head in frustration. "I think we need an expert to come in. Where does this begin?"

"This morning," the guard said, taking the footage back before the blip. "I think whoever murdered that girl wanted to hide their tracks."

"Have you been in this room all day?" she asked seriously

"No," he admitted sheepishly. "I had to go on patrol earlier."

She made an annoyed sound and stopped herself from pointing out the obvious. His patrol didn't do any good, and it would've been better if he'd just stayed in and watched the screens.

The footage went back to the previous evening and a flicker of movement caught Cecily's eye. She made him rewind and pause. A familiar face showed up on the screen. The woman looked jittery and kept looking over her shoulder. Then, she took a deep breath and let herself into Vince's room.

"No way," Cecily breathed out in shock.

CHAPTER 7

The imposing woman in the designer suit tapped her foot impatiently against the metal table in the interrogation room. She looked around in annoyance, brushing her fringe away from her face. To an impartial observer, she might've looked mildly annoyed or even impatient.

To Cecily, who was standing behind the two-way glass watching Lara Holland, the older woman looked spooked. Cecily wasn't sure when it started. Her people-watching habit. She tilted her head to the side as if she was a bird considering its prey.

Maybe it was all those years living like a guest on someone else's property. You had to watch out for when you overstayed your welcome. Or maybe it was her father's volatile temper. Or her mother's negligence. Either way, it meant that she spotted details most people wouldn't even notice.

For example, most people would've noticed that Lara had a propensity for ugly designer dress suits. Which rich trophy wife would opt for the out-of-style garments when much better pickings were available? They might even notice that she wore a white suit to her son's wedding.

An insult to the bride, and a woman who should have better style. Most people would glance over that and move on. Not Cecily. She noticed the way Mrs. Holland kept tugging at her left sleeve. This meant a few things to Cecily.

It meant that Lara was right-handed. Probably a useless piece of information. It would be filed for later. Sometimes that came in handy, most times it didn't.

It meant that Lara was self-conscious. That she wished she had more clothes on. Something thicker. Did that mean that Lara wished she had more of a shield against the world?

The list could go on and on. The point was that Cecily threw herself into the study. Her eyes flicking over every detail of Lara's mannerisms and appearance, trying to pick the thread that would unravel the imposing woman. When you went looking, you'd always found something.

This was a lesson she'd learned the hard way all those years ago. It was also the reason why she resisted going into the interrogation room for as long as possible.

"We can't keep her forever, you know," Adam said, walking up behind her.

"I thought you were working on your murder board?" she said, turning to look up at him. Only when he glanced down at her hand did she realize that she was chewing on her thumb nail. She smiled self-consciously and lowered the hand.

"I've got most of it down," he said with a proud smile, stepping out of her way so that she could catch a glimpse of the cork board he'd wheeled in after Lara showed up.

It was something to be proud of. He'd managed to create three separate categories with the faces or names of the necessary people pinned to the board. The three categories: suspects, POIs (persons of interest), and witnesses, were all connected back to a picture of Rachel.

At the bottom of the board, he'd started a timeline. There were notes of everything they knew so far. While evidence and clues were linked to individuals with different colored strings.

"What do you think?" he gestured grandly, "Will we catch our guy?"

"I don't know," she joked, "maybe we need more string."

"Very funny," he gave her a disapproving glance, but looked back at the board with a little frown.

"There's enough string," she rolled her eyes at him. "you did a good job. All I can think is that we're lucky you're in the police. With skills like that, you would've made a good stalker."

He scoffed at her again but held his hands up.

"Come on, let's get more evidence for the board."

"Is that the only reason you're doing this?" she asked as he ushered her out of the room. "For the board?"

"It's the biggest perk in the job," he said, winking at her before opening the door to the interrogation room.

Lara Holland looked up immediately and narrowed her eyes at the pair. She thrust her chin out haughtily and furrowed her brows, the picture of aggrieved socialite.

"Do you know how long I've been waiting?"

she asked, her voice tinged with anger. "I thought you were here to help us, not lock me up forever."

"Poor choice of words," Adam winced, shaking his head as he sat down. Lara looked at him in shock, but he didn't elaborate.

"I'm sorry for the wait," Cecily said sincerely, looking around the room with a light shudder. She knew better than most how this room could tug at your sanity if left alone for too long. She also had the unique privilege of probably spending more time in this room than anyone else previously interrogated.

"Yes, we don't get a lot of money around here, so our equipment sucks," Adam rolled his eyes. "it took forever to get these printed out."

He casually tossed a file full of photos to the middle of the table. Lara pursed her lips and interlinked her hands together, but she didn't take the bait and open the file.

"What is this?" she asked bitterly. "Is this your way of asking for donations? I've got news for you. Your little fundraiser isn't due for another seven months. We can talk about it then."

"We get a fundraiser?" he asked curiously, a look of pleasant surprise crossing his face. "I love small towns. They're the best."

"Adam," Cecily nudged him lightly. She gave him a stern look and he nodded profusely.

"You're here, Mrs. Holland, because you're a suspect in a murder investigation."

As a wealthy woman in a prominent family, she knew how to hide her emotions. She knew that any flicker of the wrong emotion could send tongues wagging and stocks plummeting. She was like a queen in a fishbowl court. People would circle her, looking for signs of weakness.

There were those who were looking for an easy way to make money. For her to invest in their dying businesses. Or maybe they had stocks in her family's business and wouldn't hesitate to pull out, leaving them in crisis.

She was also a woman with secrets. Which, if found out, could ruin her and everything she'd built. It was lonely and cold at the top. Eventually the cold numbed everything out and her kind would go to extraordinary lengths to feel something again.

Unfortunately for her, no amount of experience or practice could've prepared Lara for that moment. To her credit, however, her face only showed intense shock for a few seconds before she shut it down and regained her composure.

"Now I'm sure you've lost your mind," she

scoffed. "where would you get a ridiculous idea like that?"

Adam looked at her sympathetically before pushing the file toward her. He nodded at it, before she finally reached out (her hand ever so shaky) and took the first photograph.

This time, she was prepared for the shock. She looked over it primly, perhaps not even really seeing herself in a silk nightgown, slipping out of Vince's room. She put the photo back, her expression unreadable.

"I don't see what that has to do with anything," she said, raising her chin proudly.

Cecily's eyes softened as she studied Lara. She'd found her thread. It would bring her no pleasure in unravelling it.

"It was always Vince," Cecily said softly. "wasn't it?"

Lara looked at her strangely but didn't say anything.

"He wasn't always a slobby drunk," she continued, watching Lara carefully. "he must've been very handsome once upon a time. And I imagine, with his family, very charming too. What changed?"

Lara kept her silence, but she looked away

from Cecily. This time she didn't bother hiding the emotion in her eyes.

"Lara," Adam said sternly. "you need to start talking. You know how bad this could be for your family. What were you doing in his room last night?"

"I-" she started, but then Adam cut her off.

"See, I have a theory," he leaned forward, "I think you couldn't change your son's mind about his new bride. Someone everybody knew you didn't approve of. As the day came closer, and nothing was changing, I think you got desperate. I think you went to someone who felt the same way you did and decided to make the problem disappear."

"Don't be ridiculous," Lara's eyes bulged angrily.

"Am I being ridiculous?" he challenged. "Or is that what happened? I think you lured her out. It had to be something big to get her to that spot in her pretty dress. You knew how scared she was of you. That's when Vince popped out and hit her over the head with that log. Then the two of you carried her back and got back to your place just in time."

"That's not... I didn't..." Lara sputtered, looking at him in confusion.

"Tell us what really happened," Cecily said softly, making eye contact with her. Lara's gaze latched onto hers and she nodded hesitantly.

"I met Vince first," Lara gulped. "I had a massive crush on him, but I didn't know he felt the same until years later. He never made a move, but James did. Everyone disapproved because I was so much older. By the time James married me, I was already considered past my prime."

"Is that why you were so hard on Rachel?" Cecily asked softly.

Lara gulped again, before looking away guiltily.

"Partly," she admitted. "the truth is that I was jealous. It wasn't easy for me, so why should it be easy for her?"

Cecily leaned back, biting her tongue as Lara's admission sank in.

"I knew she wouldn't be able to handle the pressure. Think about it, detective," Lara turned to Adam. "I had training, experience, and I came from a good family. If I had trouble, then it would've been impossible for a girl like that. She was from a blue-collar family! How would she possibly survive?"

"She would've," Cecily said, "if she hadn't been murdered."

"I beg to differ," Lara said with a sneer. "she was already cracking under the pressure. You know where she was last night? Boozing it up with her old friends. I bet she would've run away if James and Wen hadn't dragged her back. From what I hear, they practically had to drag her in by her hair. This life would've eaten her alive."

"You're so far removed from reality. You don't think the other side has just as many problems?" Cecily said in disgust.

Lara gave a humorless chuckle and leaned on her forearms.

"We have ten thousand five hundred and thirty-four employees," Lara said in a dead tone. "all of them looking to us to pay them. How many families do you think that is? We have to keep multiple businesses afloat in this economy, with sharks looking for a way to sink us. Besides that, I have people watching me every second of every day that I leave the comfort of my own room. My husband has a mistress with a child that he'd rather spend his time with," Lara continued, her face becoming tenser as she spoke. "You tell me how a girl from downtown with twelve dollars in her bank account is going to handle that kind of pressure. Especially if she was already buckling."

"You could've helped her," Cecily said unfazed.

"you could've reached out and been the help that you never got. You could've made the future better."

"Besides," Adam piped up. "you weren't handling the pressure either. You had an ongoing affair with your brother-in-law. And who knows what the two of you did to that poor girl."

"We didn't do anything to her," Lara snapped.

"I wish I could believe you," he said unconvincingly. "but the two of you have motive and opportunity. And we found a whole lot of evidence in his room."

A knock sounded at the door, and before Adam could say anything, a harried deputy stuck his head in the room.

"I'm sorry, sir," he said, sweating nervously. "but James Holland is here to fetch his wife."

Lara looked up in shock, then quickly grabbed Cecily's hand. Cecily winced as she looked at Lara's panicked face.

"You're talking about motive, think about James. He has the same motives," Lara gulped in panic as her eyes widened in realization. "and he's much stronger than I am. Don't let him get me."

CHAPTER 8

Cecily looked at Lara in shock, unsure of what to do or say. It only took a moment for her to snap out of it, and when she did, she stood up with a determined expression. She nodded at Lara who still looked worried.

Adam looked between them with a worried expression then turned to look at the deputy.

"I'll go see what he wants," Adam decided. "stay in here."

Lara sank back into her chair then closed her eyes and lowered herself in her chair. Her face looked almost peaceful when she put her hand to her forehead.

"Why did you marry James if you were in love with Vince?" Cecily asked gently.

Lara scoffed and shook her head. It was the way she did it that bothered Cecily. Older people, especially those with privilege, had the gift of the condescending head shake. As if their problems were the only ones that mattered. That younger people couldn't possibly know anything about the machinations of the universe.

Cecily would've been offended if she hadn't realized that it was a coping mechanism. Lara was projecting her feelings, trying to hide behind a wall of condescension. She didn't usually get much attention, or love. That's why she didn't know when to be vulnerable with people. She only knew how to protect herself and so that was her default.

"Try and explain," Cecily asked, trying to keep her tone neutral.

Just because she understood, that didn't mean she accepted it.

"Vince was charming and handsome, but he didn't have a head for business," Lara said with a sigh. "around the time we got to know each other, his business was failing. His pride couldn't take it, so he turned to the drink. I couldn't rely on him, and he never asked me to. That's when James came into the picture."

"And you made the smarter choice," Cecily guessed.

"What else was I supposed to do?" Lara barked. "I was past my sell-by date. Vince never asked me, and I decided to do the smart thing."

"What about love?" Cecily asked slowly. "Why didn't you approach Vince? I'm sure he could've used you when he was down."

"Love doesn't last," Lara scoffed, rolling her eyes. "it's a child's notion. I needed security, and James offered that. Besides, why did I have to be there for Vince? He would've sucked me dry and taken me down with him. He turned his back on me. What was I supposed to do? Force my way in? No."

"You could've told him the truth," Cecily pointed out.

They heard raised voices from outside, and Lara flinched. She looked back at Cecily, her nerves turning into iron.

"I chose my path, and I helped build an empire," she said proudly. Then she reached for her handbag and stood up. "I'm not ashamed of my choices."

"You can't leave yet," Cecily protested. "you're still being interrogated."

"I think you'll find that I can," Lara paused

strategically to let her husband's voice filter through the door. "unless you charge me, you can't keep me here. And good luck trying to find a judge to sign any kind of warrant. Who's the nearest judge? Judge Myers? I'm sure you can find him with all the other guests."

With that, Lara seemed to have regained her confidence. She turned on her heel and headed for the door.

"Did it last?" Cecily asked. She was about to let the other woman go when she noticed Lara tugging at her left sleeve.

Lara paused at the door, then turned back to Cecily.

"Did what last?"

"Your love for Vince," Cecily explained. "you said that love fades. But did your love for him fade?"

Lara lingered for a second longer, before ducking out the door and letting it close behind her with a soft thud. She didn't have to say anything. The answer was written on her face.

Cecily decided against following her, and quickly checked her messages. A few from her friends came pouring in, but one made her stop. It was from Marianna. It was a warning that came a little too late.

James Holland is on his way with a cease and desist. I'm warning you - they're our biggest clients. Do whatever he says.

Her heart sank as she read the message, then she got up and quickly went to join Adam.

It was clear that he was fighting a losing battle. On one side was the Holland family. James at the helm, poking his finger at Adam's chest while the rest of the family seemed to hide behind him. An unfamiliar man with thick glasses stood nearby with an expensive briefcase. Cecily guessed that it was the family lawyer.

On the other side, Adam stood all alone. His jaw was squared, and he had an angry frown that indicated who was winning the fight.

Cecily squared her shoulders bravely before walking over to stand on Adam's side. He glanced at her briefly as she stood next to him. It wasn't much, but she knew he was grateful for her support. As she looked up, she caught sight of Marianna.

Her cousin-in-law looked away, frowning defensively. Cecily had a feeling that this wouldn't be the last time they'd be on opposing sides.

"You're to drop this witch-hunt against my family, or there will be consequences," James was saying. His face was contorted into a snarl, and it wasn't hard to imagine him murdering Rachel.

"Is that a threat?" Adam asked carefully.

"I don't need to threaten anyone. I'm just giving you a friendly warning," James said, with a shrug. "you can't harass my family like this. The girl's death had nothing to do with us. If anything, you should be asking her family. They were a rough crowd."

"We're investigating a homicide," Adam said patiently. "we have to interrogate certain people. Your wife had several public arguments with our victim. We're not harassing you; we're following procedure."

"Here in Pleasant Valley we have our own set of procedures," James said. "you better wise up or get out."

"Correction," Adam said, gritting his teeth. "you used to have your own set of procedures. Not anymore. Now, you have the law. Same as everyone else."

"We're simply using our rights, officer," James said, sneering at him. "if you want to talk to anyone in the family, our lawyer has to be present. And another thing, you can't lurk around the hotel trying to ambush us anymore."

"The victim was murdered at the hotel," Adam protested. "it's an active crime scene!"

"No, the room and the corner of the property are active crime scenes. The rest of the place is off limits, unless you have a warrant."

James seemed to sense he had won the argument, but he looked more furious than smug. It was probably the first time a public servant, or any kind of servant, had taken a stand against him before. James Holland was a powerful man, but he was also like a spoiled toddler. Things always went his way, or he threw a fit.

Unfortunately, his tantrums had real-world consequences for his enemies. Right now, Adam was turning himself into James' biggest enemy.

"Step down, officer," James said, stepping closer so that their noses were almost touching. "you don't know what forces you're messing with."

He looked back at Marianna who gulped and stepped forward tentatively.

"He's right, you can't conduct any more interviews on the estate, and you'll need a search warrant to search through any other areas."

"You're kidding," Cecily scoffed. "I'll never agree to that."

"You don't have to," James sneered. "we also

own shares in the estate. With Marianna on our side, you're outvoted."

"You sold these people shares in our house?" Cecily asked in disgust.

"It's not our house," Marianna said defensively. "it's a business. And this is how businesses are run. I'm sorry to burst your bubble."

"You're as bad as they are," Cecily told her, glaring at her business partner.

"You can't keep harassing them."

"Oh boo-hoo," Cecily said, rolling her eyes. "poor rich people are uncomfortable. Tell that to Rachel. Someone snuck up behind her and hit her with that log. She didn't stand a chance. You know how old she was? Twenty-four. She had her whole life ahead of her."

"What happened was tragic," James said, sounding unaffected. "but it's not our problem."

"Not your problem?" Cecily asked, gasping a little. Her eyes were round with fury now, and she didn't care that her words caused Marianna to go green. "If it weren't for you people, she'd be alive and happy. You keep talking about how she didn't deserve to be in your family, well you're right. I wouldn't wish that on a pig!"

"Cecily," Adam said firmly, taking her arm. "that's enough."

"I hope the money's worth it," Cecily spat at Marianna who was visibly cringing. "I hope it'll soak up the blood."

Adam sighed heavily, and she quietened down, glaring reproachfully at the Holland family.

"We'll keep these restrictions in mind," he said, nodding slowly.

"You better learn your place," James said imperiously, before turning and walking out.

It didn't take long for everyone else to clear out, but it was enough time for Cecily to calm down and quickly think of a plan.

"I'm going," she told Adam, grabbing her handbag from the nearby chair where she'd left it.

"Wait a second," Adam grabbed her arm. "I know what you're going to do."

"Don't try and stop me," she warned, rounding on him furiously.

"I'd never," he said with a smirk. "we just have to be smart about this."

"Is this why you got so calm so quickly?" Cecily asked tilting her head. "You've got an idea?"

"Well," Adam said mischievously. "that, and I got a text from the medical examiner while you were yelling at them. Good job, by the way. You really let them have it."

She looked away in embarrassment. She didn't regret what she said to the Hollands. In fact, she wished she could've said more. She just wished that she hadn't lost her cool. It seemed so much more satisfying telling them off in a low, calm voice. Unfortunately, her voice had gotten all high-pitched and she was afraid of bursting into tears.

That's the thing about strong emotions. It would be so much more effective to let them loose while staying stoic. But that's not how they work. They also have a physical element, which can be taken for hysteria or overreacting.

Cecily knew that James didn't take anything she said to heart. He probably dismissed her as a hysterical female. A part of her wished that she could sit him down and carefully explain what the world thought of him. She smiled slightly to herself.

That imaginary scenario would take place in her daydreams. She couldn't wait to make daydream James cry his eyes out. She was also certain that she wasn't the only person who'd had such fantasies before.

"What does it say?"

"That log didn't kill Rachel," Adam said with a sigh. "apparently, she was suffocated."

"What?" Cecily asked in shock. "But… there was so much blood."

"Yeah, the head wound would've been fatal if it wasn't treated, but she had time. Someone made sure that she was dead."

"Why do you look so satisfied?" Cecily asked in annoyance. "That changes everything."

"Yeah, it means that we need to find a pillow-case full of make-up. The ME says that the killer probably used a pillow of some sort. And we know where to look now. The Hollands wouldn't slap us with a cease and desist unless they were hiding something."

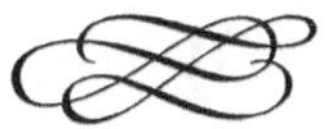

CHAPTER 9

Walking back into the hotel felt like sneaking back home after curfew. There was a strange sense of exhilaration that caused Cecily to slip quietly in through the front door and sneak back into the kitchen.

By now, several guests had found their way back into the kitchen and some had taken slices from Cecily's grand masterpiece. The pink inside of the cake contrasted with the snowy white frosting. Several iced flowers were drooping sadly, as if they guessed what had happened.

Cecily looked at it, her heart sinking a little as she thought about what should've happened today. If everything had gone according to plan, then Rachel and Wen would've been opening the dancefloor. Their song was "Can't Help Falling in Love" by Elvis. A little cliched, but it summed up their situation perfectly.

After grabbing a pair of plastic gloves from the cupboard, Cecily made her way out of the kitchen, giving the cake one last look before closing the door behind her. She felt her phone vibrate in her pocket and she sped up her steps.

She knew who was messaging her and why. It wouldn't help answering until she found what she was looking for.

It wasn't hard to break into Rachel's room. Picking the lock was a piece of cake. After all, these were the doors she practiced on when she was a kid. This was the easy part, and possibly her favorite. It was the thrill of accomplishment. Cecily took pride in whatever she did. When she put her mind to something, she worked until she perfected it. This single-minded determination meant that she had quite a few interesting skills up her sleeve.

The hardest part was stepping through that door and knowing what had happened in the room. Rachel spent her last moments in that room. She'd come in with so much hope. The walls had seen something horrific and now they'd be telling that story every time Cecily came in.

You're losing it, Cecily told herself. It would be easy to fall into romantic daydreams about the room, but the truth was that the room was just a room. She repeated this to herself as she started searching methodically through everything.

The crime scene techs hadn't had much of a chance to sweep through everything yet. They were understaffed and underfunded. They'd get to it when they got to it. Despite the Hollands' influential name, the process hadn't been sped up. Cecily suspected it was because James hadn't asked them to.

She opened the cupboard doors and crouched down when she saw something interesting. There, nestled underneath the complimentary bath robe, was a little overnight bag. Cecily opened it gingerly, expecting to find Rachel's honeymoon bag.

Instead, she found ordinary clothes. She was about to dismiss it when she noticed that a pair of jeans had a slight bulge in the pocket. Inside, was a plain white envelope. It was folded so many times that it looked old. The seal had been broken, indicating that someone opened it after it had been sealed. Her hands shook lightly as she opened it.

Darling –

I'm sorry, but I can't do this anymore. They were all right. I'm not cut out for this life. I know I promised you I'd try, but you also made promises you couldn't keep. You said this would be easy. This isn't a fairytale anymore, it's a nightmare. I should never have agreed to this. It was wrong. It was so wrong. I made a mistake.

I love you. I do. But if you loved me then you wouldn't ask me to do this. How can I do this to another person? Why couldn't I be enough for you? Why did you have to ask me to do this? We were happy, weren't we? Don't you remember the picnic by the beach? You brought champagne and we stayed up all night talking? It was so simple then. I would've done anything for you. Did you plan to use me like this? Is that why you asked me to do this terrible thing?

They kept saying how I wouldn't understand this world. They were right. I don't. How could you use me like this? I never wanted to be a part of this stupid, twisted game. You ruined my life. And if I stay, I'll never be able to fix it. I'm a real person. I'm just important as all of you.

I wish I'd realized this sooner. You don't love me. You never did. If you did, you wouldn't have done this to me.

Don't follow me. Leave me alone.

Cecily lowered the letter in shock before

quickly dialing Adam's number. They spoke for a few seconds before she got to her feet and rushed over to Wen's room. She knocked once before pushing the door open.

Inside, Wen was sitting on an armchair with his legs folded and his hand over his mouth, while Doug stood by the open window smoking a cigarette and Trish was pacing in front of the fireplace. They all looked up in shock as she entered.

"We didn't order any food," Trish said, looking at her incredulously.

"Rachel was going to leave you," Cecily said hurriedly, ignoring Trish.

Wen looked up at her with a frown, his hand still in front of his mouth. She held up the wrinkled letter and his eyes widened with surprise. Then he shook his head slowly.

"She wasn't going to leave him," Trish scoffed. "she was just throwing a little temper tantrum because Lara made her sign a pre-nup. She thought she was going to get her paws on the fortune."

"I wasn't talking to you," Cecily said dismissively, focusing her attention on Wen. "I can't imagine how embarrassing it would've been for you if she had left you by the altar. After all you'd done for her? I can imagine how angry that would've made you. Did you find out what she was planning to do? Is that why you called her out and killed her before she could do it?"

Trish let out a scandalized gasp, then flounced out of the room, slamming the door behind her.

Wen scoffed derisively and rolled his eyes. Doug crossed his arms worriedly and breathed out a plume of smoke. She turned to glare at him. He held up his hands in surrender and blew the rest of the smoke out the window.

Wen gestured at his friend, and Doug stepped forward and handed him a cigarette. He lit it up, breathed deeply and glared at Cecily.

"Cute story," he said in a raspy voice. "but I didn't kill her."

"You didn't mean to kill her. And when you saw what you'd done, you panicked. So, you dragged her back to the laundry room, stuffed her in a cart and pushed her all the way to the room. Then you staged the body and ran down to the venue."

"Once again," Wen said, rolling his eyes. "cute."

"What did you do to her?" Cecily asked, narrowing her eyes at him. "She must've been furious to write this."

Wen pursed his lips and didn't say anything.

"I saw you drag her into this hotel," Cecily

said, straightening her shoulders. "I know you weren't gentle. It wouldn't have been too hard for you to hit her over the head."

"Seriously?" Wen asked in annoyance. "What do you want from me?"

"I want to know the truth," Cecily said, grabbing a chair and sitting across from him. "you play the part of a grieving fiancé, but she was scared," she waved the letter at him. "she was terrified. What did you do to that poor girl?"

"I didn't do anything," Wen said with a frown. "I don't even know what that letter says."

Cecily thrust it at him. She saw Doug start forward, but then think better of it and step backwards. She looked up at him curiously. He looked away and took a drag of his cigarette. Wen let out an annoyed sound and thrust it back at her.

"This wasn't for me," he said in annoyance. "we never had a picnic at the beach."

Cecily took the letter back with a look of surprise. The gears turned in her head as she tried to figure out what happened. If this wasn't for Wen, then who was it for? If it had been opened, then there was a good chance that someone had already read it.

She jumped in fright as she got a call, then

something clicked in her head. She reached into her pocket and switched off her phone.

"You said she went outside because someone called her," Cecily said slowly. "but what if no-one called her. What if she was the one who called them?"

"That's ridiculous," Wen spat. "Why would she meet someone in her wedding dress?

Cecily was so focused on Wen that she didn't notice Doug's look of terror. He blinked rapidly then quickly took another drag of his cigarette. Meanwhile, Wen was done with his and put the butt in the ashtray. She looked down automatically, but when her eyes saw the brand, her eyes widened in realization.

She looked accusingly at Doug who stamped out his cigarette and ran his hand through his hair.

"Because she knew she wasn't going to marry you," Cecily realized. "she never wanted to go through with it. Someone put her up to this, and she wanted to back out. That's why she wanted to meet up with him. To tell him it was over, but he needed that money, so he tried to make her stay. When she wouldn't, he killed her."

"What?" Wen asked, obviously getting irritated. "Who are you talking about?"

Cecily lifted her chin and nodded behind him. Wen turned around in annoyance, his face going slack when he noticed Doug's expression.

"What did you do?" he asked in horror.

Doug looked away guiltily. He breathed out heavily and sat down on the corner of the windowsill. A slight breeze blew through the window. As he sat there, Cecily realized how a young woman like Rachel could've been enamored with him. He looked like the hero in a historical romance. Unfortunately for Rachel, he was more like the rotten villain.

"You set this whole thing up," Cecily accused. "she wasn't the one trying to get her hands on their fortune, it was you."

"Why?" Wen asked, his voice getting high-pitched. "Why did you do this to me?"

"I didn't mean for anyone to get hurt," Doug said pleadingly. "I'm desperate, okay? All I needed was for you to invest in my business. I knew your father would never do it, so I had to get creative."

"Creative?" Wen spat. "I loved her! She was everything to me!"

"Everything?" Doug scoffed. "You treated her like she was dumb! I saw you bully her. You're so desperate, you would've taken anyone."

"Not anyone," Wen sneered. "remember, I sent your sister away."

Doug looked like he was about to launch himself at Wen, but then he thought the better of it and turned away.

"I didn't mean to kill her," Doug said, his tone lifeless. "all I wanted was to stop her. I didn't want her to leave me. I didn't mean to hit her that hard!"

"Well,' Wen said, desperately looking for some way to hurt his friend the way he'd been hurt. "she was going to. She didn't love you either."

"That's where you're wrong," Doug said with a sigh. He sat on the ledge, angling his body toward the air outside. "I'm the only one she ever loved."

Before anyone could stop him or guess what he was about to do, Doug pushed himself out the window. Cecily gasped and looked away, covering her ears before she could hear what came next.

CHAPTER 10

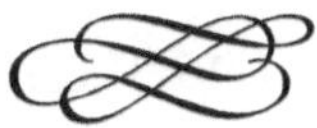

After the ambulance had sped away, Cecily turned to Adam with a tired sigh. Marianna was outside, busy ushering away all the curious onlookers. James and Lara Holland were nowhere to be found and it seemed that, for the moment, they weren't going to be sued for anything.

"Thank goodness he only broke his leg," Cecily said, rubbing her eyes slowly. "I can't imagine the trouble we'd be in if he killed himself."

"Well, he's going away for a long time now," Adam said grimly. "I can't imagine a jury's going to have much sympathy with him."

Cecily nodded, kicking the ground lightly with her foot. They had a lot of cleaning up to do before they could put this whole thing to rest, but something was niggling at the back of her mind. Something felt off about the whole situation.

"You know, I just don't get it," Cecily said slowly. "Doug really loved her. This was a crime of passion. He hit her over the head, he didn't lure her outside. I really don't think he planned any of this."

"What are you saying?" Adam asked in confusion.

"This is a murder in two parts," Cecily told him, squinting up at him as she thought. "the initial attack happened outside. It was brutal and unplanned. Like any crime of passion. Then, she was taken upstairs and staged. We know someone probably put a pillow over her face. Like, they wanted her dead and wanted people to find her."

Adam nodded slowly, scratching his chin as he thought.

"Okay, let's think this over," he told her slowly. "Rachel asked Doug to meet her outside. She tells him she's leaving him. He gets upset, hits her over the head. She falls to the ground, and he probably panics. What does he do?"

"Say what you want about Doug, but he really didn't seem smart enough to handle something like that on his own," Cecily said thoughtfully. "I mean, the idiot jumped out of a third-story window and thought it would kill him. I really don't think he was the mastermind behind all of this."

"Right, so when the plan fell through, he probably called the mastermind behind all this," Adam said, snapping his fingers knowingly. "I'll call the station and ask them to get all of Doug's phone records. He probably made the call right after he hit Rachel."

"Great," Cecily said, suddenly feeling lighter. Her gut told her that they were on the right track.

TWO DAYS LATER, CECILY WAS BACK BEHIND THE two-way glass, watching Rachel's murderer talking to the family lawyer. She looked at Adam with determination and they nodded at each other. Adam opened the door for her and together they made their way to the interrogation room.

"I'd just like to say that my client won't be answering any questions that she doesn't have to," the pudgy man with the round glasses said haughtily. "she won't be tricked by your questioning."

"We don't have any tricks," Adam said honestly. "we've just got facts. Trish, stop us when you feel like it."

She smirked smugly at him and leaned back in her chair.

"We'll lay down the facts," Cecily said, putting her folder down on the table. "and you can stop us when you feel like confessing." She paused and gave Adam a meaningful look before continuing. "Fact one, your brother was left in charge of the family business when your father died, but he wasn't good at his job and lost millions."

"The company was bleeding money and investors were pulling out in droves," Adam continued when she paused. "you needed a cash injection, but no-one was going to be stupid enough to invest with Doug in charge. Unless you had someone on the inside."

"Fact two, you're smarter than you look, but you're also extremely lazy," Cecily said.

"Objection," the lawyer glowered at her. "that's slander."

"I'm sorry," Cecily said with a wry smile. "you don't like having to work for a living. Doug met Rachel in college, then when they met again sometime later, they fell in love. Around that time, you realized the business was dying so you tried to jump ship by marrying into a rich family. Unfortunately, everyone knew what was going on and no-one wanted you. You got so desperate, you even tried Wen, but he spurned your advances."

"Rachel was working a party that Wen attended, and when you saw him staring at her, you got an idea. Thank goodness you convinced Doug to keep his relationship with her a secret."

"Fact three," Cecily continued. "you convinced your brother to ask Rachel to pretend to get together with Wen. If they got married, then you'd be able to use her to get his family to invest in Doug's company and save it."

"You knew you had to play the part of the disapproving family friend, but it was so easy to make Rachel's life difficult."

"Fact four, Rachel wanted to leave the whole thing behind. Her conscience was bugging her, so she decided to leave both Wen and your brother. She called Doug and told him it was off. He got so angry that he hit her over the head with a log. Then, he panicked and called you. The mastermind behind this whole debacle."

"That's when you two carried her into the laundry room, hid her in a cart and took her back to her room. You made Doug hide the bloody log and towel in Vince's room because you knew he'd been out all night. While Doug was gone, you realized that Rachel was still alive. You couldn't help yourself, you put the pillow over her face and pushed. It took a while, but when you were done, you staged the body and dumped the pillow in the laundry cart."

"That was one of many mistakes," Cecily said, shaking her head sadly. "you've never done laundry in your life, so you didn't realize that you can't machine-wash a pillow. The maids found the right pillow almost immediately. We tested the case, and surprise - your DNA was all over it."

"You're joking," Trish said with a snort. Her lawyer looked at her in panic, shaking his head at her. She ignored him and continued. "if what you say is true, why would I kill her? She was supposed to be helping me."

"That's true," Cecily said, nodding slowly. "she was supposed to, but she didn't want to anymore. You couldn't risk her telling the truth. It would destroy whatever dignity your family's reputation has left. Besides, you hated her. She was a dock-worker's daughter who managed to get a man who turned you down. You didn't think twice about putting that pillow over her face."

"You had motive, opportunity, and we have

more than enough evidence to convict," Adam said matter-of-factly. "we have the pillowcase, and the phone records. Don't worry, they'll teach you to do laundry in prison."

"If your case is so solid, then why am I here?" Trish challenged, her skin going pale behind her fake tan. She folded her arms defensively and looked between the two of them with wide eyes.

"We don't want you making this harder on the family by pleading not guilty," Cecily said point-edly. "we want this done, and a signed confession."

"Good luck," Trish scoffed. "I'm innocent, and I'm going to fight this thing for years."

"How?" Adam said with a frown. "Your family is out of money, your brother is already in prison and we've got mountains of evidence on you."

"Besides," Cecily said with a shrug. "we've got a signed confession out of Doug. He's saying that you're the one who told him to kill her. The way things are looking for him, he's about to get off with five years, while you're going to be put away for life."

"What?" Trish screeched, slamming her hands on the table.

"Trish," her lawyer said, going pale. "don't listen... It's ..."

"That little worm!" she screamed, her face going red. "He did everything! He hit her! If it weren't for him, we would've gotten away with this! He's the one who ran the business into the ground. If dad had left it all to me, we wouldn't be in this mess and he'd still be with that stupid girl."

"Why won't you tell us what happened?" Adam asked slowly.

"I'll tell you the truth," she spat. "but only if you guys help me get a deal." Adam nodded slowly. She breathed deeply then launched into her story. "I was getting ready for the ceremony when that moron calls me, blubbering. He managed to kill her, he thought, when we were minutes away from winning everything. I walk over there, and she's in her dress. There's mud and blood everywhere."

"Trish," her lawyer said urgently. "stop. Please. They're tricking you."

"He's crying in the corner, and I've got to fix everything again. I get him to help me with the body, but he's such a mess he keeps dropping her. Then, I tell him to hide the log, but he takes forever because Lara's also in Vince's room. He had to hide until she left. When he finally came back, Rachel was busy waking up."

"He knew she was still alive?" Cecily asked in horror.

"He started panicking and talking crazy. He said they were going to run away together and live happily ever after." She stopped talking as she rolled her eyes in disgust. "Rachel took one look at him and started screaming her head off. I wanted to get her to keep quiet, but she wouldn't listen. That's when I realized she was never going to let us get away with it."

"So, you took the pillow and made her keep quiet."

Trish nodded slowly, looking away quickly. Her lawyer let out a pained groan and laid his head on his hands.

"You absolute idiot," he moaned. "you're going away for life."

A FEW DAYS LATER, CECILY WAS MIXING BATTER for that night's cake when a strange man walked into the kitchen escorted by Marianna. Cecily didn't notice they were heading toward her until it was too late.

"Cecily," Marianna said in her soft Australian

accent. "there's someone here who wants to meet you."

Cecily looked up in surprise, quickly wiped her hands and looked at him curiously.

"I'm Rachel's father," he explained, extending his hand for her to shake. Her eyes softened and she reached out to shake his hand firmly. "I just wanted to thank you for what you did for my daughter."

"That's okay," Cecily said kindly. "she deserved justice."

"And I'm glad she got it," he said in his gruff voice. It was clear that he was a dock worker. From his rough clothing to the hands that were leathery from years of hard work. "I told her this world would eat her alive, but I guess she wanted more out of life than we could give her."

"Oh," Cecily said in surprise. "I'm so sorry, sir. But she wasn't in it for the money. I think she did it for love. She knew what she was doing was wrong, so she tried to fix it. That's the only reason she got killed. She was doing the right thing."

Rachel's father blinked unexpectedly. He looked down, his eyes teary.

"You don't know how much it means to hear

you say that," he said, trying to keep the tears at bay. "she was just doing the right thing."

He nodded at her, then slowly turned and walked out the kitchen. Cecily watched him walk out the door with a strange lump in her throat. She knew it was worth it. And that she'd do it again.

AFTERWORD

Thank you so much for reading A Deadly Wedding.

I'd really appreciate a review on Amazon.

Look out for Book 1: The Murdered Heiress which is now available on Amazon:

The Murdered Heiress

Please join my newsletter to stay in touch with all my new releases:

http://eepurl.com/c0Bv5b